I would like to tha helping me to reac to help guide me through to writing my first novelette.

My Mother, for being strong and always there for me. Supporting me throughout.

My best friend Marie, for being the life and soul of the party, bouncing ideas left right and centre.

My partner Bill, for getting me to knuckle down and finish my writing. The sunshine in my life.

To all I thank you from the bottom of my heart.

      Jet xxx

Time To Die By Jet Hipwell

Chapter 1   The river

Chapter 2   Too close to home

Chapter 3   Too much talk

Chapter 4   Dark days

Chapter 5   Not going to plan

Chapter 6   Party party party

Chapter 7   Not long to go

Chapter 8   The woods are calling

Chapter 9   Murder at midnight

Chapter 10   That was unexpected

Chapter 11   All is well?

Chapter 1 - The River Bank

Along the river bank the sun began to set. Tall woodland trees secluding the small camping spot, placed perfectly in the clearing. A small tent for shelter and a roaring wood fire for the evening's heat, as Jet and Sarah sit supping cider from cans, laughing and relaying past history like they were teenagers again. The calm waters can be heard beneath the rustling of the trees, as dawn approaches Sarah breaks the laughter with a more serious line of conversation.

"So the big C has got me good Hun. You know I'm going to die right?" The question left open and unanswered. "I want you to help me! Die I mean." Jet looked perplexed and shocked at the statement. "Chemo hasn't worked, Radiotherapy didn't work, fuck even the herbal bullshit didn't work. You know I even tried a voodoo healer." She laughs as if there's no care in the world.

"Jet, come on, you have to help me. I don't want to end up a vegetable, in pain and gasping for my last breath. Let's do something mental, go out with a bang, or at least something that will make me drift to sleep and not wake up. I don't want to go through all that pain and trauma, and I know you know how to do that stuff. You're like Miss Herbalist 101 down there." She laughs again looking longingly at Jet for an answer. "No one even knows we are here."

Sarah Christian had been suffering with thyroid cancer and battling for over a year now to survive. At thirty six she had suffered a long life of eating disorders, heart problems, medication overdoses, and endless lines of self harm and mutilation. Hospitals and specialists around the country all failing at easing the suffering, and after several failed attempts at therapy she had made the choice to end her own life. Jet remained quiet as she stared intently into the flames. Sarah not even realizing that Jet had already thought long and hard about euthanasia, and had already made up her mind on the matter.

"So will you help me?" Sarah said all big smiles and doe eyed. Jet pondered on the words and replied rather cryptically.

"Dude you know what I probably will" She laughs and retrieves two more cans from the hamper. "For now we drink and party, it's just us and the woods baby. Just us and the woods." They both begin to howl at the now slowly rising moon, laughing and drinking long into the night.

After the night of teenage antics both Sarah and Jet settle down for the night, sleeping bags tucked up tight and a small headlamp illuminating the tent. Sarah being exhausted was the first to fall asleep, Jet however could not get the thought of killing someone out of her head. Mumbling to herself "I have the perfect solution right here in front of me." Rattling around in her overnight bag, producing a hypodermic needle and a vial of clear liquid. It was pure fast acting insulin, one hundred millilitres exactly. Jet knowing full well that when her blood sugar was in the thirties and high off the meter scale, a mere sixteen units would bring her back to normal. Having been diabetic nearly all her life, she knew that the astronomical amount of insulin would cause diabetic coma and death.

"She's already asleep... It's what she wanted" Jet whispered to herself slowly filling the syringe full to the brim with insulin. "I considered this for myself too once you know, it has to be a peaceful way to go surely?" Sarah slept peacefully beside her, totally unaware that this would be her last time to dream.

Unzipping and pulling back the sleeping bag Jet slowly exposed the top of Sarah's body, rolling the cover down Sarah stirring gently, rolling onto her front, and exposing the top side of her ass cheek. "Perfect" Jet muttered, breathing in slow and deep she placed the syringe over Sarah's skin, gently pressing down the needle went in with ease, as the plunger went down slowly the liquid begins to disperse, until all one hundred units were gone. Jet releases the syringe and covers Sarah's body with the sleeping bag, keeping a close eye on her breathing, as the insulin would take twenty minutes to half an hour to take effect.

Knowing what she had done, Jet could no longer sleep, her mind racing in a million directions. Sitting outside the tent back at the fire Jet contemplates the idea of why she doesn't feel upset. "I have just killed my friend... yet I feel nothing? What the hell is wrong with me?" At that moment a loud coughing and gargling sound came from inside the tent, Jet racing to see what's happening. Sarah's body was convulsing and twitching, an off white foam oozing from one side of her mouth. With one last rattle and a huge gasp she was gone.

"Fuck!" Jet is now panicking slightly. "Dude I'm so so sorry. It was meant to be peaceful, not like this." On secondary panic Jet then checked for a pulse. She was definitely gone. "Now what the hell do I do with you?" Again Jet shocked herself at how calm and unemotional she felt. "Hmmmm I have a river... River leads to a small lake. That will do nicely." Collecting her bag and basket of food Jet started to clear the tent, all contents outside baring that of a dead body. Removing the poles one by one the satin-like dome collapsed in on itself, covering Sarah's silhouette. Tired and adrenalin hyped Jet then rolled Sarah's body up in the tent, adding stones as she went around, once tied up with guide ropes and filled as much as she could with weight, Jet then made her way to the river bank dragging Sarah's body along the grass, so as to not rip and tear the fabric.

At the water's edge, again the thought popped into her head. I murdered my friend and now I'm disposing of the body. "What the hell?" She said aloud as she rolled the body into the water, slow and steady the orange bulge began to sink and bubble, as it sloped into the depths of reads and marine plants. The ripples and bubbles take a while, but eventually they come to a stop, leaving only the woodland noises and the sound of the river. "I killed my friend, but that's what she wanted, and Jesus I don't feel bad about it" Jet headed back to the camp site as rain slowly started to come down, killing any remaining remnants of the fire. Collecting her belongings and filling the rucksack she headed for the short walk home.

As she arrived home the thoughts started to swirl. Throwing the camping gear into the porch and heading straight for the kettle, a strong warm brew was needed. Do I have no heart? She thought to herself, stirring the contents of the cup, and reaching for the tobacco pouch in her back pocket. After the smoke was rolled, Jet sat at the dining room table. "I need a brain dump. Where's my diary?" Jet often sat and wrote for hours, using the pages to clear her head of any unwanted thought or emotion. Looking up at the clock it read 2am... The phone rings.

Chapter 2 - Too close to home

2:15am The taxi had made it in good time, hoping she wasn't too late. Jet had known her father was going to die, another victim of cancer that couldn't be cured. Heading into the hospital she was led round corridors and corners, reaching a large set of double doors. "He's in there," a nurse calmly said. On entering the room the smell of chemicals and death filled the air, John lay out on a bed writhing in pain, gasping and pleading not to die. The horrific scene was broken by the words of Sue, his wife. "It's ok John, it's your time to go now. Be in peace" Fuck that Jet thought to herself.

"Hey. Dad, I know you can hear me. How come you get quiet machines eh? Mine used to make horrible noises." They both laughed, a glimmer of acknowledgment that he knew who his daughter was, and that she was there by his side. Sue sobbing uncontrollably in the corner, mumbling the words "Please dear god just let him go". Jet reaching out for her father's hand, and leant close into his ear. "It's ok Dad I'm here, and I love you" With those words spoken John took an almighty gasp, the air gargling in his throat, and expelling long and slow into the air. An eerie wave of silence filled the room, broken by the sound of Sue's voice. "Do you want a lift home?" She said tearfully.

"I want a minute with my Dad first." For god sake woman. Jet thought, he's only just passed and you want to get home to the bottle already.

It was late now in the early hours of the morning and jet was pacing up and down the kitchen, scrolling through social media trying to take her mind off the evening's events, when she came across a post that stopped her in her tracks. "What the actual hell" Sues profile had been set to widow but that was not the shocking part. It was a post between her and another man joking about cocktails that very morning. "I knew she was going to buy a bloody puppy, but a new man?" Sue was one of those women that couldn't stand to be alone for more than ten seconds, without hitting social mental breakdown levels. Stories told by her other children call of men being put before them, even down to the evil bastards that beat and nearly killed her. Jet had to know, instantly messaging her step sisters to see if her suspicions were correct. Sadly they were.

Within the week of John's death, Sue had managed to buy a sports car, two pedigree pooches, decorated the entire bungalow, and found herself a new fella. She doesn't waste any time, Jet thought. "The woman has no respect for the dead or the living" She said to herself. "I want her to pay for the wrongdoing of her children and the disrespect of my father. I want her dead!"

Over the course of the next few days, this entirely occupied and overtook Jet's thought process. Finding out that this new guy was not only NEW but an evil manipulator as well. Within one week the entire contents of Sue's life were signed away to him, hideous tattoos had marked her skin, and talk of marriage was already in the air. All Jet could think about was how much they deserved each other, and battling with the thought. Can two birds be killed with one stone?

One year to the day, on the anniversary of her father's death, Jet was preparing the nightclub for a regular weekend, her brain fuelled with anger and rage. Not coming to terms with her dad's passing, and feeling the anger of Sue not having a care in the world about her own kids, something had to be done, and the present feeling was that she could be the only one to do anything about it, although having had a year to stew and ponder on it, the plan was made ready and waiting. Sue and David were going to die on their honeymoon.

The honeymoon was all planned and booked, one week self catering in traditional Spain, it was a small chalet in the heart of Pamplona, bags were packed and ready to go days before leaving, only they were missing one vital bottle of Glenfiddich for the holiday. Sue heads out to the shop to get it while David sleeps off his dinner in the other room.

Jet had slowly been collecting and saving a concoction of both Sue and David's medications. Several illnesses such as depression, heart problems and other such things meant that the pair of them were on some pretty high powered stuff, and jet had prepared a large bag of mixed pills, crushed into a fine powder, enough to kill a small elephant, but she had to make sure it worked. Sue returned, removing its proud green casing, packing the bottle gently into the top of one of the suitcases. As the evening went on after a couple of drinks she began to fall asleep on the sofa, Jet eagerly biding her time, and once both were asleep this was her chance.

Retrieving the bottle Jet poured out a small amount, enough to take the amount of powder about to go in. It fit snugly, the cap was replaced and the contents shook vigorously, before wiping down and replacing the bottle in the bag, Jet slid an envelope to the bottom containing a joined suicide note from the pair of them, and the bottle went in on top nicely as it had before. "And now I wait" she said to herself, gathering her things and collecting her coat, leaving both victims asleep on the sofa, "See you on the other side assholes." She laughed while exiting the bungalow knowing that this may or may not work, but if she had planned everything right neither Sue or David would bother her again, and knowing they would down the bottle together in one night, meant that it was a sure fire way to get them to drink the same amount.

The return date arrived, but Sue and David did not. Jet checked the flights; they were not on any other later ones either. Has the plan worked?

One week later Jet received news from her step sisters, saying that the wicked witch is dead and so was Dickhead, these being the loving nicknames given to Sue and David by the other four kids. It's odd we were discussing news of the deaths yet all of us were happier somehow a weight had been lifted from us all. There was no love loss here, and Jets instant thought. "My god it worked."

Later that evening Jet's mind was racing, thoughts of what she had done, and what she had gotten away with. Killing a friend that's already dying is one thing, but killing your step mum and her fella is another thing entirely. Thinking of Sarah at that point there had been no news, over a year had gone by and nobody missed her, or even knew that she was gone. The cancer would have killed her by now anyway so I guess that makes it alright. She thought to herself. "No evidence. No crime. Right?" She laughs, "I still have no emotion, no pain, guilt or fear about what I have done. I still sleep soundly at night. Does this make me a monster? I need to talk to someone. There was literally only one person in the world that she could talk to, that wasn't about to judge her for killing three people. That was her best friend of a lifetime Marie Spellman, she only lived a twenty minute walk away, so it was time to pay her an unannounced visit, a quick text would have to do.

Chapter 3 - Too much talk

Marie Spellman was the best friend and double act to Jet, complete opposites but ultimately best friends. Marie was tall and beautiful, but had a quirky flare to shock all. No verbal filter. This blunt honesty and humour was what Jet loved about her. No bullshit approach to everything. Sat across the kitchen table, brews made, smokes rolled Jet began to tell Marie the events of what had actually been happening over the last two years, although they spoke every day, and saw each other twice a week, Jet had chosen to keep quiet about the three counts of murder, until now.

"Holly shit! I can't believe you got away with it. That's mental Jet... Just mental. So let me get this straight. You killed a lass no one misses, she was dying and wanted to die anyway, so you put her out of her misery, and you killed two inconsiderate assholes that deserved it... Hmmm I don't see a problem with this somehow."

"You have to promise not to tell a soul. I mean it Marie you can't tell anyone about this."

"As if I'm going to tell anyone this is madness, but I tell you what, if you want proof I will keep quiet, I will go in on it with you."

"Eh, how is that possible? They are already dead."

"Nah mate I'm talking you help me bump someone off too... Sure you won't have a problem with it when I tell you who and why." She cackles at the thought. "You remember Shell Web? Here's a quick rundown for ya if you don't. She had her dog put to sleep because she couldn't get anyone to look after it. She's been pregnant three times, and had all children taken off her. She's a drug addict and an alcoholic, and to top it all off she's pregnant again... Sorry for the rant but she's right royally pissed me off... What do you say? One more scumbag off the streets. You remember her now, right?"

Without thought or hesitation the answer shocked Jet herself.

"That would take some serious planning, and at least a fresh brew." They laughed as though this were some episode of CSI they were discussing. Marie clicks on the kettle.

"So let's do this, me and you we can make this work I'm sure."

"She's an alcoholic for a start that makes life a little easier; she's always off her face too, so no one will bat an eyelid if she has a fatal accident." They laugh, Jet unsure as to whether or not Marie is serious, something in her gut instinct tells her it's true.

"Let's get on to another subject. Have I told you what my mother has done... again!"

The two go on into long conversation, a three hour bitch fest about everyone and everything that's pissed them off that week.

"It's getting late. I best set off and walk home." Jet suggested.

"Yeah that's not a bad idea, I want to have a hot bath and sort my stuff out for work tomorrow. I shall message you in the morning for a brew and a smoke before I go."

"Ok then darling I shall talk to you soon." As Jet started down the street, she suddenly realised in the cold air that it had already gone dark. Reaching into her pockets and finding a pair of gloves she shivered putting them on. Three streets down music could be heard blaring from a house party, yelling amongst singing and lights, there was definitely an argument of some sort on the street. As I got closer to the corner I could see the small block of council flats, lit up like Blackpool illuminations with disco lights and loud rap music. A voice comes from out of the dark.

"Oi Jet you coming up?" The voice was no other than Shell Web, as if that wasn't freaky enough she was inviting me to the party. It was then I saw the opportunity. Shell standing there, in her forties hanging round with all the scumbag kids of the town, full on tracksuit socks tucked into the trainers, hair scraped back from her dishevelled face. The years have not been kind to Shell, but drink and drugs probably had a lot to do with that. She stood at the top of twelve hard concrete steps, with concrete walls either side courtesy of the council's best efforts, to stop vandalism of what once stood metal railings.

Thinking of this, I realised I had been walking forward and was now at the bottom step.

"Long time no see." Shell slurred. All I could think about was those poor kids, and her beautiful dog. The things that Marie had reminded me she had done. I reached the top step. Shell looking heavily pregnant and ready to drop, yet highly intoxicated on whatever concoction the night holds. Previously all her children had been born with problems, and taken directly into social care.

"Want a pill?" were the next words out of Shell's mouth, and I saw red. A quick glance around told me there was no one else around outside, and she was so close to the edge of the step, swaying left and right. "Well? You going to party or what?" The question went unanswered as I pushed firm and hard in the base of her back, the bag of pills flying everywhere. Shell hit every step on the way down, smashing her head against the sides and colliding in a heap at the bottom, head bouncing one last time off the curb.

"Shell?" I said quietly with no reply. Heading down the steps to what was now forming a large pool of surrounding blood, I quickly checked the pulse, and she was dead. Looking around again hearing the noise of the party raging inside, I knew someone would come out soon. "Think Jet... Think." With no apparent onlookers, I quietly walked away and headed home.

The next morning I awoke to my usual video call with Marie, she seemed very excitable.

"Jet, have you seen socials yet this morning?"

"No, I have literally just woken up." She said laughing. "I'm going to make a brew."

"Before you do anything, get yourself online... Dude Shells DEAD!" not able to contain herself she squeaked.

"Really? What happened?" I asked, knowing full well the answer.

"She took a load of pills and fell down the flat stairs silly cow, we don't have to do anything now."

"We don't have to do anything. You're right there... But I already did." Jet said, winking at the camera.

"No waaaay, you didn't?"

"I did. One hard push, and walked away." So simple and no one will know any different bar us. So again I repeat. DO NOT TELL ANYONE!"

"I won't, pinkie promise." They continued to discuss the details over a morning brew and a smoke, Jet constantly thinking how unbelievably easy this has all been, and how she still has no feelings of guilt or remorse. Jet turns to Marie on camera.

"I think I'm going to jump off for a bit and clean the house now Hun."
"Yeah me too, and just think while you have your tunes on cleaning, you can be thinking about who's next." She cackled in a rather evil way. Maybe she was right. I had kind of got the taste for murder.

Chapter 4 - Dark Days

Dear Diary,

I'm confused... I awake each day with no feelings, no dreams, no emotions... I killed people, like it was nothing, feeling no remorse, no guilt. I'm not even frightened by the consequences of being caught. What is wrong with me? This is so not normal, although Marie seems to think it's somehow cool, I don't think she has fully thought it through. We are two oddballs that are truly bound by friendship, and now murder... Hmmm writing all this down is probably not a good idea either, one sure fire way to get caught... Hmmm fire. This will be my last entry before the flames engulf my words.

Jet looks onward, deep into the reflection of herself in the mirror.

"For Christ's sake your nearly forty woman" I look young but I feel old, my mind is a mess, a contradiction of everything in life. What is emotion? What is love? They say actions speak louder than words, but what if you have actions with no feelings? Words are empty, but actions are hollow. I wish so much for my health to be improved, yet it never seems to change, every step I try to make better only retreats three steps backwards. Hospitals, Counselling, Specialists and Doctors. No one makes anything better, even a multitude of medications can't put me right. "What is wrong with me?" Marie was right though, there are plenty of people that have wronged me in life, and the way I feel right now I could happily kill them all, but one name sprung to mind. Matt Fielding.

Matt was perfect. One of many failed, short lived relationship attempts, only this guy was a real piece of work. Not that I knew it at the time, but he turned out to be a master manipulator, a complete narcissist, drug abusing alcoholic. Each day spiralling into an intoxicating world of heroin and booze, topped off with any legal pharmaceuticals he could get his hands on. "He scares me... He is next." With those words Jet picked up the diary snapping it shut, and headed off into the garden where a previously prepared fire pit stood central, pouring some lighter fluid over the book she began to set the pages alight, throwing the whole thing into the sticks and kindling that instantly caught light. "Goodbye." She whispered, watching the flames dance around. This would take lots of thought and planning, but no pens or paper. It was video call time, if anyone could come up with ideas it was Marie. How? What? Where? And When?... Hmmm she thought as she began to dial her number.

"Helloha how are you? What can I do you for?" Marie asked.

"Stressing (laughs) I need some ideas bouncing, are you on your own? I have decided who's next."

"Ooooo. Let me make a brew and roll a smoke, and I will be right with ya. Let me guess. Is it Matt by any chance? Because he would be my first choice."

"No way! It actually is."

"I knew it would be haha. I thought about it last night and came to the conclusion that if anything, that evil, dirty little scrote deserves to die. Although if you ask me, we could just beat the shit out of him and leave him where he lays, people will just think drug addicts did it."

Matt Fielding was a forty one year old Heroin addict, with the charm and mysticism of the best. He could literally sell ice to an Eskimo, and charm his way into any girl's pants with talk of ancient wisdom, mystical stories and smooth talk. However in the world of the living this guy was a ghost. Anonymous socials, cryptic names, and constantly moving home.

"So ok, we start with the question. How do we find the ghost?" Jet well happy that Marie was totally on board with this.

"Only way we can find him, wait and see." She laughs. "He's always hanging around town or at the chemists for his medications. I'm actually going to have to do some surveillance on this one, and that's quite hard considering how I look. There is tons of CCTV in town, and at the chemists."

"Let me do it." Marie said bright eyed and bushy tailed, like a small kid at Christmas. "No one knows me or what I look like round there, I can suss him out for you."

"Hmmm ok. So what's the plan if and when we find him?"

"Once a dirty addict always a dirty addict. We hot shot him. Wait for him to get home and take his stuff, then when he's out of it, stick him with the rest."

"You really have given this some thought." She laughs hard.

"You have seen him cook up and take it before, so all we have to do is copy that. Right?"

"I guess so yeah. How do we judge how much to give him? How much heroin kills someone?" You see we don't know these facts. I can't just Google it"

"All of it!" She laughs wildly. "If he's bought brown for the week on payday, we wait till he's had his dose, then we hot shot him with the rest."

"I love the way you say that so calmly and without a thought. Although that plan may actually work. So I take it you're doing surveillance, and lookout?" Jet is now laughing at the thought.

"Yeah I'm up for this. I'm going to watch him and his crackhead mates for a week, then we will know the ins and outs of when it is best to strike. I shall start by following him home, so we know where the current crack den is he's living at. He's never too far from the chemists." Both now laughing at the fact that all this seemed so easy.

"You do realise there is no going back from this. Once done it makes you an accomplice to... Oh fuck... I'm technically a serial killer."

"Life is shit right now for everyone, so I have no regrets. You killed Shell and she deserved it, so I'm with you on this one. Matt deserves to die. The guy thinks he's God and above everyone else, he's hurt so many people along the way, so many good people have died and yet that scumbag still lives, he's a waste of oxygen."

"You're totally right Hun. You do your thing, and I will work out the rest, we can discuss it in a few days. Good luck." Both exchanging blown kisses and goodbyes. The plan was in place.

One week later – The phone rings. It's Marie.

"Hey Hun, how are you?" Jet answered.

"Sooooooo I got all the info we need. I got an address; Tuesday is payday, all the crackheads go out at once to collect the money around 10am. Matt is the first one to get home, we have about an hour's window till the next bunch return. I looked through the window, he's pretty out of it for most of that time, and all the stuff we need is in a shoe box under his bed."

"Wow you really did a thorough job at this, well done. I have made up some herbal fast release poison to go in the mix, and a hypodermic syringe. Half and half should do it."

"Well it's Thursday now so we have time to wait, I assume you are heading to the club for deliveries, and set up."

"Yeah I am just getting my stuff ready as we speak, it's payday weekend so going to be a mad one, I will be well knackered when I get home."

"Well rest up well Monday as Tuesday is going to be busy." She said laughing.

"Right well on that note my lift is here, so I shall say goodbye and I will see you Tuesday."

"It's a date." The phone hangs up, as a car horn can be heard from outside. Jet grabs her gear and heads for work.

Chapter 5 - Not going to plan

Tuesday morning arrives as the alarm rudely awakes Jet from her sleep, shortly followed by the ringing of the doorbell. Again the doorbell rings.

"Ok ok I'm coming." Jet shouted.

As she opens the door half asleep Marie comes bursting in.

"How can I use my key if you leave yours in the door woman? She laughs.

"It's 6am dude. I am not as bouncy as you. I need a brew and a smoke."

"Make a thermos mug and smoke on the way, we need the first bus to town if these plans are going to work. So chop chop, get a move on." The stuff was prepared the night before, Jet's handbag held the key to killing Matt Fielding.

The bus arrives in town not far from the chemists itself, Marie and Jet don't have far to go to reach their destination. On arrival there was already a line of people waiting outside, and sure enough fifth in line was Matt, hunched over and smoking a spliff, music blaring from his phone, annoying everyone else in line.

"So now we wait. Good job I brought the thermos it's freezing." Jet opens the canteen and they share a warm brew whilst biding the time. As Matt exits the chemist grounds, they stay far behind keeping him in line of sight, but not close enough to be seen. Arriving at the flat. If you can call it that. It was a shared accommodation, consisting of drug addicts and thugs, corridors strewn with needles and foil, the dank smell of vomit and urine filling the hall. Matt's room being ground level meant that Marie could keep a look out, and report back what was happening in the room. After ten minutes a text came through... You're GOOD to go!

Jet slowly opened the door to the room, knowing that he never locked it. That was the first part done. The room itself was disgusting, a basic bed surrounded by drug paraphernalia, alcohol bottles and bowls of sick. This truly was the worst I had ever seen him. Matt was laid out on the mattress, no covers or quilt, just stains of various kinds. He was completely out of it, not even wake-able by shaking. Marie could just be seen outside the window, concealed by a small bush. I was already ready to go; I didn't need to search for anything. The heroin, foil, spoons and other bits were already laid out on the bed next to where he lay. Syringe in hand I approached his body.

The needle was half prepared with a herbal concoction of poisonous roots, berries and leaves, now for the second part. Taking a large tablespoon out of her bag, she proceeded to burn what remained of the heroin into liquid, and carefully filled the syringe to the brim. Flicking and shaking its contents, tourniquet around his arm and veins pumping. The nerves were making her hands shake and sweat in the latex gloves, as she saw Marie mouth the words "Do it!"

The needle went in without a glitch, slowly pressing down on the plunger the contents were dispersed into Matt's arm. Jets phone began to vibrate... Someone is coming back, the text read.

"Shit!" Jet said. It vibrates again... HIDE NOW!!!

A male voice could be heard entering the building. "Matt dude can you lend me some cash?"

There was literally nowhere to hide. Two options under the bed, or in the wardrobe, knowing Matt had very little belongings or clothing with him, most of which were on the floor. Wardrobe it is she thought to herself, as she quietly stepped over the carnage that covered the floor. Narrowly jumping into the old wooden wardrobe, only to find that the door was damaged and therefore didn't entirely shut. Holding on to the door as tightly as possible from the inside, she heard the male enter the room. He then spoke again. "Matt, Dude, wake up, I need some cash." Matt's body remained lifeless although still breathing. Realising he was out of it and wouldn't wake up, the guy started to go through the box under Matt's bed, rooting through he seemed to find what he was looking for, and maybe more, as he chuckled to himself filling his hoodie pockets. He then turns and leaves the room, door wide open. The phone vibrates... Go NOW! Running for dear life Jet shot out of the room and through the corridor, slipping on something on the way out. Marie grabs her hand.

"You did it mate." She shoves Jet down behind the bush. "I will take a look... He's foaming at the mouth face down choking... No wait... The movement has stopped. I think he's dead."

"How the hell do we know? I mean he should be. How long do we wait?"

"We don't." Marie said, grabbing her hand. "We walk now." Pulling her back away from the window Jet could see there was no one around. "Ok we walk." Arm in arm like any other day, Jet and Marie headed back to town for the long bus journey home.

"I can't believe we did it. The scumbag is dead, and he can't hurt anyone else. Did you pick up the stuff on your way out?"

"Yes, the syringe and tourniquet are in my bag. I am going to put them in my sharps bin at home, it gets collected next week, then goes off to be incinerated, the rubber gloves can go in the fire pit, so that's the evidence gone."

"What did you mix in it?"

"A bunch of stuff but mainly foxglove, that way if he survived it he would have tripped balls, and would have no clue what had happened. As it stands the plan worked and he is gone for good."

"Wait. Foxglove isn't that the pretty flower in your garden. The tall one with tubes for petals?"

"Yeah (Jet laughs) Pretty but highly poisonous in the right form. You can make LSD from it, but the wrong amount will stop your heart, so it's not worth playing with, stick to your shrooms." The pair laughs uncontrollably. They had been chatting so long they had hardly noticed the journey go by, and the bus was just pulling into the yard.

"This is us. We made it home." Marie said. "How long till someone tells us he's dead?"

"Someone at the club will mention it, one of his cronies no doubt."

"Brew?"

"Brew." They nod at each other in agreement.

Walking through the door Jets phone rang, it was a young lad she knew from her old DJing years, only kept as an acquaintance of the bar, thanks to him going down the road of drink and drugs, due to his actions he was now currently barred for six months.

"Hey Jet it's Dez, long time no see, just ringing with some bad news but I thought you would want to know that Matt's died, he OD'd earlier today."

"Why are you telling me? I have nothing to do with him anymore."

"He once said you were the only person to ever show him kindness, and had a true heart. So I guess I thought you would want to know."

"Well thank you for telling me."

"Ok sorry to have bothered you this evening with such bad news."

"The only way you would know what happened is if you were still in that lifestyle Dez. I take it your back on the hard stuff?"... The line went dead.

"Well news is out already, that was quicker than I thought. Again though, we got away with it."

They smiled at each other drinking the last of the tea, Marie pipes up. "Well thank you for a really eventful and exciting day that dickheads gone and we can sleep peacefully at night." The two laugh. "We should do it again sometime."

"For now stay safe, and let me know when you get home."

"I will beautiful. Goodnight." Kisses are blown and the door closes.

Jet exhausted makes her way to bed, doing the usual routine of; Teeth - Toilet - Time. Once the alarm was set, she settled down watching the stars of the bedside lamp rotate, as she thought to herself... "My God. I'm an actual serial killer... And I'm good at it." With that said, she drifted off to sleep.

Chapter 6 - Party Party Party

Several months had gone past without any crazy antics or killing sprees, just normal everyday life. The club was struggling due to the corona virus outbreak, and Jet knew it may not survive into the New Year. Trying to hold on to the positives in life, she had been invited to Marie's end of summer BBQ Party in a week's time, where everyone would be having a great time, drinking round a fire, great food, and getting doggy playtime with Bruno. Bruno always cheered Jet up no matter what kind of day she had, the dog was always happy to see her, giving love and cuddles with a rather excitable tail wagging. That thought made her smile. The phone rang.

"You must be psychic. (Jet laughs) I was just thinking about you and the BBQ next week."

"Well it's about that, that I want to talk about... Do you fancy helping me out with something?"

"Always Hun if I can I will help, what's the problem?"

"My Mother." Marie said, laughing her head off.

Karen Spellman was a nightmare. Totally selfish, not giving a damn about anyone except herself, mutton dressed as lamb, supposedly suffering from anxiety and depression, however watch her turn up to every party going. Not only that the woman was a full blown alcoholic in full denial, and Marie would always be the black sheep of the family in her eyes. Not being able to push out grandchildren fast enough, like the rest of the herd meant that Marie was singled out, and not given a damn about. Something told me I knew what she was about to ask.

"Can we bump her off please? She's way worse than anyone else you have killed, and this is personal. She's done it again. Lied about my age to her friends to make herself look younger, only she got caught out because one of them spoke to me about it. She tells everyone that she comes to see me regularly, and that our relationship is all hunky dory. When really the last time I saw her was last year, when I got dying garage flowers for my birthday, and she drank half my liquor cabinet, cracking jokes about not getting more grandkids. I have even done the hard part for you; I have collected a full strip of all of her medications. If we use the pestle and mortar to make them all powder, and then whack it in whatever bottle she has concealed in her handbag. People will just think she's over done it again on her meds, and messed up big time. Do you think that will work?"

"Seems legit if you really want to do this, you keep her busy and I will tackle the handbag bit. Might be hard though she always has it on her."

"Not until she's done drinking everyone else's booze first. (She laughs) She won't bring any to share for the party, but she will drink whatever other people bring, till it runs out. So until she needs her handbag, I can hang it with the coats, and you can run it upstairs to the bathroom to put the stuff in, while I keep her busy."

"You realise she will die in front of everyone, and someone will call an ambulance."

"Yeah but she will have made such a fool of herself by that point, no one is going to care or say anything other than she is pissed as a fart on her medications."

"Ok bring the pills round and I will see what I can do. I shall crack the kettle on."

"Beautiful. See you in fifteen."

Marie and Jet talked the morning away. Marie telling all the humiliating stories about her mother and what she gets up to, at these parties she would try and act like all the younger people, and be necking booze quicker than anyone could pour it. There were stories of neglect and misconduct amongst the children, and lack of care for her ill father. Too busy partying and not enough care for her supposed loved ones. Jet knew she could get on board with topping Karen off, she was just unsure about it happening with such an audience. The rest of the killings had been people that were hardly missed, and done in secret, but something longed in Jet to try. Challenge accepted, she thought.

The night of the party arrived, and on Jet's arrival everyone greeted her, handing out nibbles and drinks. Avoiding all to start with she made a beeline for the dog. Bruno was sitting there wagging his tail and waiting for cuddles and love, toy poised in his mouth looking as cute as ever. Dumping her bag she made her way to the side of the room.

"Brunooooo" She said, getting bowled over by slobbery kisses and love.

"Glad you could make it," Marie said, winking at her. The majority of guests being in the garden with the food, or in the living room with Marie's other half on the games console. "She's already half pissed. You got the stuff?" She asked eagerly.

"I got it Hun." Jet replied.

"She's currently necking a bottle of baileys and trying to dance in the garden. She has already fallen over once, and the rest of the party are trying to avoid her like the plague. When that bottle is done, she will move on to the bottle in her bag, like it's the same bottle because when she put her phone away I caught a glimpse of it. So you have about twenty minutes until she does."

"Ok so let's get it over with, which handbag is it?"

"The only one big enough to carry a bottle." She said laughing. "I hung it on the banister, just watch out for the people in the room."

"I'm on it!" Jet jumped up into action and headed for the stairs. The large handbag could be seen on the end of the railing, but people could also be seen in the room to the right. Jet's hands began to shake a little; she sat herself on the bottom step and removed her trainers, before grabbing the handbag and heading upstairs to the bathroom. Finding a flat surface Jet removed the bottle of Baileys from the bag, cracking open the seal around the metal cap. Pouring a dribble down the sink she then filled the bottle with the powdered mixture, a small amount spilling on the side.

"Dam." she said to herself, grabbing some toilet roll and dampening it with water. Once the spillage was cleaned up, tissue flushed down the toilet and hands washed, she wiped down the bottle and replaced it into the handbag. Giving that a once over with a baby wipe and heading back downstairs. The party was going strong and most people were in the garden now as food was being served, Jet placed the bag on the banister, and wiped the handle down. It was done. She could now enjoy the party.

About an hour later Marie came over with a drink, passing her the bottle she said. "Just a heads up. Mums gone for the bag." The two of them walking into the kitchen could see Karen sliding the now empty bottle under the counter. "You alright mum?" She asked.

"Yeah! You?" She slurred back.

"Always." Marie laughs. Karen now wobbles back to the garden. "See that's as much conversation as she's had with me all bloody night, she just doesn't care about anyone but herself. I can't wait to see her finish that bottle." Looking across the garden Jet could see Karen drinking straight from the bottle, in large glugs. "Now we wait." Marie said, staring across the yard.

After some time had passed people were noticing Karen complaining of feeling sick, there was nothing new there, a few people took her a chair outside by the fire and told her to sit down, she was also taken several glasses of water, all of which were refused in place of the bottle, and the party carried on around her, It was at that point Jet noticed the bottle slip from her hand to the floor. Is it done? She thought to herself.

As the party was winding down one of the guests suggested that we shouldn't leave Karen out in the cold. "Just chuck a blanket on her like normal." One of the crowd replied. A blanket was brought from inside and taken up the garden. It was then we heard the scream.

Karen was sitting in the garden chair as if posed like a doll. Her face gray in the dying fire light, and a huge globule of white foam sliding down her chin. "Call an ambulance!" One of the girls shouted. Marie and the others ran up to see what was going on. One of the bystanders went to check Karen's pulse; only on touching the skin did she proceed to slide off the chair and onto the floor. Hitting the ground with a hard thud, her body then began to convulse and shake. With a huge gargling gasp she was gone.

Blue lights flashed on the driveway, neighbours curtains twitching from left to right, to see what is going on, as Karen's body was loaded into the back of the ambulance, after the ME pronounced her dead at 11:45pm

Several weeks later the report came back as alcohol poisoning, with a high level of pharmaceuticals in her blood, resulting in a final heart attack. The phone rings.

"Oh My God! We did it! The bitch is dead, the rest of the family are acting like they care but they don't, they just want to know who's getting what." She said laughing wildly. "Even my Dad's health seems better now the stress of her has gone. We did goooooood Jet. We did well."

"Well I am happy your happy Hun, I'm having a down day today, not sure why just feel very empty inside, personally lonely I guess." Jets voice low, and saddened.

"Awwww Bless ya Hun, do you want me to come round for a bit and keep you company? We can have a smoke and a brew. I also have cake." She said laughing.

"Well if there's cake then definitely." She said laughing back. "I will put the kettle on."

Chapter 7 - Not long to go

"Wakey Wakey." Marie's voice sounded from downstairs. As I glanced at the clock it was 10:30am I had overslept my alarm. "I have come for a brew; I shall put the kettle on while you wake up."

"I'm alive." I shouted back. "I forgot you were coming this morning, I have overslept." (She laughs) Throwing on a dressing gown, and heading downstairs to the kitchen. "Jesus it's cold this morning, trees are starting to go orange and red too. It looks so pretty." She said looking out the window.

"Brews on the table." Marie gestured to the chair. "Sooooo who's next? Life is crap right now and I'm bored of all the shit people keep throwing our way. I need some excitement in life. Come on. You know you want too. Let's make the next on a mystery, or leaving people puzzled" She said laughing loudly. "Something fun."

"Hmmm ok, but we stop at seven victims."

"Why?" Marie asked impatiently.

"Because of many reasons." Laughing together Marie squeals.

"Are you going to tell me these reasons? Or do I just have to guess?"

"Seven because it's my lucky number. I have seven piercings in my right ear. I am the seventh grandchild in the family, and if we carry on we will get caught." Jet said, looking deadly serious.

"Ok Ok I get it."

"That's the problem with serial killers. Leaving evidence, not thinking it through, murdering with your heart and not with your head. Telling people. Too many murders..."

"Yeah I get it. You're the great serial killer and I'm just the sidekick." The sarcasm oozing from her words. Yet she still seemed upbeat about it all.

"So this one has to be special, and exciting if it's our last. We really need to think about who deserves it the most, and what we will have to do to achieve it."

"So the question is... Who do we kill?"

After several hours of debate, the decision had been made to murder Rebecca Price. The girlfriend of a long-term close friend Lesley Ballard. Rebecca was controlling, in every sense of the word, not to mention half her life didn't seem to add up. She quickly drove a wedge between Lesley, Jet and Marie, even though they had been friends for years. The talk of engagement happened just weeks after they met online, and more and more secrecy crept in. Paranoia and recorded or listened into phone conversations were soon happening and a massive argument in a group chat over something entirely childish rocked the boat even more. Jet and Marie siding on one view point, and Lesley and Rebecca firmly on the other, and communications between the group had ceased.

"So how do we kill her exactly? You're the one with all the crazy, make it exciting ideas, what do you suggest we do?" Jet said ready for whatever crazy ass ideas were about to come out of her mouth.

"How about we stab her to death... No! Wait; hang her from a tall tree... Maybe both." She said laughing at the thought of Rebecca swinging in the breeze.

"Hmmm ok you said trees I can work with that. How easily do you think we could get her on her own for a camping trip? To get to know us better. Maybe do a bit of ghost hunting, story time, that sort of thing. It's not quite winter yet we can have a fire and marshmallows, lots of blankets kind of idea."

"That sounds amazing. Not just for murder. Can we do that regularly?"

"Maybe. It does sound like fun, but in this case we string her up in the trees, make it look like an occult murder... You wanted excitement and puzzles, only this puzzle cannot be solved."

"Oh my God. I love it. This is going to be so much fun, we need to start preparing. I will work on getting the idea in Rebecca's head that it's a good idea, then if we are all systems go you can sort the camping gear, and I will sort the food stuff."

"That's fair although we will need other provisions to. The woods up near the old manor house ruins will be perfect, and it's not far from here. We can walk an hour or two if I pull the camping trolley."

"What if we leave evidence?" Marie said, suddenly worried.

"Of course there's evidence of us there, we were all camping together. By the time someone finds her, she will be decomposing in a tree, and half eaten by animals. It's so remote out there and quiet I doubt anyone will find her for ages, and besides when she goes missing, we are the survivors. We join the search parties... No one is going to go up there to the woods, if we say we were camping near the ruin. They will be searched eventually but like I said it will take them a while, and she will be well chewed up by then, there are plenty of wild animals in those woods, especially foxes, and those hungry buggers will eat anything."

"Ok and what if they do find her quick? Just saying."

"Then some crazy occult dickheads snatched her while she went to pee in the night, and we never saw her again."

"Jesus this seems well complicated now." Marie's voice seemed to crack a little.

"It's not if you follow the rules and stick to the story. If you're getting cold feet then say so now, preferably before we get to the cold woods and spend two hours building a fire, because if you crack then I will kill you, seriously I will kill you." She said jokingly and laughing gently.

"Nah I'm all good for this. I'm ready to go on camping adventures. Are we all in one big tent?"

"Yeah it's my download festival tent, it will be snug with three in, but only two of us have to sleep in it." They both laugh profusely." We will work out what to do with her, once we are in the woods, if we leave her to sit by the tents while we collect firewood, it should give me the chance to scope out the right place to put her. It's been years since I have been there, so it may be well different now, maybe even overgrown, I shall take some cutters and stuff just in case. We are headed for a small cave area in the centre of the woods, it's really sheltered by trees, so keeps the wind out well."

"Like I said, sounds like an amazing adventure camping trip to me. I can't wait."

"Remember it will have to be during whenever she next comes down to visit Lesley, and during the week, as I can't take time off work... But that in mind. Go do your thing." She laughs as Marie pulls out her phone heading straight for the socials. The easiest way to stalk anyone without them even knowing.

"B.I.N.G.O Marie sang. It's next week when she's coming down. So I'm going to message her now and get the ball rolling."

Hey Rebecca, how are you? Just wondering as we all left the group chat on such bad terms, Jet and I were wondering if you would like to come on a camping trip with us. Just us three so you can get to know us better. Drop me a message and let me know what you think? Xx

Marie then promptly thought to message Lesley and tell her that we were going camping to try and get to know her girlfriend better, and she was equally up for this as she wants us all to be friends, even though we didn't see eye to eye on the way we left things. A reply came through.

Hey Marie yeah I am good with that. When (Shrug emoji)

Next week if that's cool with you? Probably Monday afternoon, after Jet's finished work stuff.

(Shrug emoji) Yeah that's fine.

"What is it with those bloody emoji, that's what caused the whole argument in the group chat. Why does she answer everything with a cartoon shrug?" Jet asked angrily.

"I don't know dude but We Are ON! She's up for it Monday afternoon, so that doesn't give us much time to prepare."

"I will sort it. You go get your bake on, we need brownies for the trip." Marie grabs her bag, blowing kisses and heads for the door.

Chapter 8 - Woods are calling

After a good hour's walk, we all reached the lane entrance, blink and you would miss it. Easily concealing the great Manor Lodge that hides at the other end.

"Right guys we have a fifteen minute walk down this lane, and we reach the Manor. Then we have ten minutes to the woods. Jet instructed Marie and Rebecca.

"My feet hurt already, and we have another twenty minutes till we get there for god sake." Rebecca moaned at the thought of more walking.

"I don't know what you're moaning about woman, me and Jet are pulling the bloody trolley." Marie spat back.

"Remind me why I am doing this again? I know it's to get to know you better, but surely we could have done that back home." Rebecca had reluctantly said yes to the camping trip, and clearly didn't want to be there. On approaching the Manor Lodge, Marie stood in amazement.

"Wow, it's massive, and beautiful. I so wish we could go in it." Marie said gobsmacked.

The Manor Lodge stood three stories tall and proud, with large wing quarters either side. An off cream colour with a large bell tower at one end. The structure looks both old and somehow modern at the same time, as it looked nothing like the original building from the sixteenth century. This sadly burned down through unknown and unforeseen circumstances in seventeen sixty one. The remake of the building however was still impressive, although worn down over the years; the large square courtyard shaped building still had style and a haunting disposition. Surrounding this great building there were forests as far as the eye could see, and Jet was unsure as to where to go next.

"Right, let's have a smoke and a brew, while we have a rest, then we can head to the woods. It looks different from when I was a child, but I know I always used to go left from here. So if we head down what remains of the footpath, we can find a clearing somewhere to camp further in." Jet said, trying to sound like she could remember where she was going.

"Sit down and a brew is a good idea." Marie piped back. Rebecca, still looking miserable, parked herself on the grass. "We have got chairs, you know." Marie said like sitting on the floor was rude or something. She begrudgingly passes Rebecca her chair, and proceeds to get another one out the trolley for herself.

As they sit supping warm tea and coffee, Marie gets out Jet's video camera and starts recording the surroundings. Making sure to get as much of the lane and building in as she could. Knowing that her footage would probably become police evidence, she wanted it to look extra touristy.

"Right, let's get a move on." Jet said, packing her mug and foldaway chair back in the trolley.

"Roger that." Said Marie. "Come on Rebecca you don't have to be miserable all the time you know, you can smile every once in a while."

"Now now children play nice." Jet said in response. "We are nearly there."

After a good ten minute walk they reached a small clearing, next to what looked like a small cave entrance, big enough for a child maybe or a very small person to climb into. "This is where we pitch up guys, let's get the tent out and up, then we can make a fire, and get the kettle on again." She said laughing at the amount of caffeine they all drank. Marie propped the video camera up on a nearby rock, and they began assembling the tent. It was a fairly easy job between the three, and was soon standing proud, and not a single argument between them.

"Awesome." Jet said. "Right Marie! You go grab us a load of firewood and Rebecca and I can sort the camp, and get the kettle on."

"Yes Boss." Marie replied with a salute, as Jet showed Rebecca how to use the camping stove, and to get the tea prepared, she began unloading the chairs, sleeping bags, blow up beds, and other luxury camping gear. The loud whirring sound of the pump could probably be heard for miles, although surrounded by trees and bushes it would somewhat dampen the sound.

"Now that's timing." Marie said as she came back with arms full of branches and bits of woodland debris. Steam began to rise from the kettle. "Nice one Rebecca, two sugars for me and one sweeter for Jet. Don't go giving her the wrong one mind." She said laughing. Jet laughing too at the sly diabetes dig. Jet then hammered a stick into the ground a few feet away from the tent, on the surrounding edge of the camp.

"What's that for?" Marie asked curiously.

"I am going to put the camping loo, straight ahead from this pole in the bushes or behind a tree, that way in the night you only have to look for the stick to know what direction the toilet is in."

"Aaaah I see. I like that idea. Can we have a few more on the way so we can follow the sticks back." Marie said laughing. Jet laughs along.

"Sure thing ya wimp. Scared you will make a wrong turn, and the ghosties will get ya." They all laugh.

"I'm going to go for a walk to stretch my legs while it's still light." Rebecca said with a high tone of annoyance.

"Ok Hun but don't go far, it's so easy to get lost out here." Marie said, although secretly thinking that's the perfect opportunity to get things rolling. "So when she comes back, the next brew duty is mine. I will slip Rebecca the sleeping pills, then we go ghost hunting. Wherever she drops we find the nearest tree, and you tie her to it, then while she sleeps we can set up the rest of the stuff." Marie sounded excited about this, and trying hard to withhold the squeak from her voice.

"The pills are slow acting, they are just antihistamines. We should have a good two hours to ghost hunt before she drops. So make sure you have both camera batteries in the bag. My bag is already full of rope, tape and the flasks and stuff, so make sure you have them.

"I have, don't worry. We are doing this and it's going to be fun." With this said Marie started to unfold the sleeping bags and blankets, making the tent like a proper home.

The tent was now set up, with a small table surrounded by three camping chairs in the centre, and outside a little tea and cooking station, a circle of stones had been prepared with sticks and lighter blocks all ready to go, as Rebecca could be seen returning in the dusk.

"Did you enjoy your walk?" Marie said, as Jet begins to light the fire. "You fancy a brew after your walk?" Marie asked, even though she was already heading for the kettle.

"Sure thing." Rebecca replied. She had barely said a word the whole journey so far, and was refusing to act civil, or even try to enjoy the experience... She deserves to die! Jet and Marie were thinking the same thing, as a sly look at each other was all that was needed. Marie finished making the drinks, Rebecca's now containing added extras, they began to sit and talk. Planning the ghost hunt and what they were going to do. A short while later, brews down and fire is spent, Marie pipes up.

"It's starting to get dark ladies, let's get this show on the road. Camera is rolling. Jetpack led the way." With a torch a piece, and a spare set of batteries each they headed into the woods. Following a straight line for about twenty minutes, they arrived at another small clearing, this one having a large, degraded, unrecognisable statue and what looked like a gravestone next to an old oak tree.

"This is where the lady in white is meant to roam, legend has it that this is the Lady of the original house that burned down years ago, and she can't bear to leave the grounds." Jet told the tale in a somewhat creepy voice, easily getting the other two excited and wanting results.

"Oooooooooooo, it's getting exciting!." Marie squealed. "Come out lady in white!." She shouted eagerly awaiting a reply or vision. The woods were silent, and then a small rustle came from the edge of the clearing, all torches shot in that direction. There was nothing... Again Marie shouted "Come out come out wherever you are!... Whoever you are! We want to see you." On cue another rustle from the bushes, this time on the other side of the clearing, all torches spun in unison, hearts beating, eager to see this mysterious being. It was then they all clapped eyes on the elusive ghost... It was a small white bunny rabbit, bobbing around in the bush.

"Oh for fucks sake. This is ridiculous. Can we not just go home?" Rebecca asked. "I'm getting tired and I just want to sit down."

"Sit here against this tree for a while." Marie said, knowing the plan was falling into place. "You sit here and chill, roll some smokes, and we will stay here a while then go back to camp. Cool?"

Marie and Jet continue calling out the dead, spinning around in the moonlight and shining torches at every sight and sound, group hysteria was building. After about half an hour Marie noticed the cigarette had dropped from Rebecca's Hand... She was out cold.

"You got the rope Jet?" Marie asked. "Cameras now off."

"I sure have." She produced a large, thin, rope-like cord from her rucksack and quickly tied it round Rebecca's body, then securely around the tree. "Right! I will spray the pentagram and symbols on the floor. You go grab the longest branches you can find, so we can make a large pentagram for the tree. I don't really fancy defiling a nice old tree."

"We are committing murder here and you won't deface a tree?" Marie said laughing. "Ok Ok I'm on it. Large branches coming up." She said, chuckling to herself as she walked away.

Jet took out a can of pure white spray paint, and in the torch and moonlight, did her best at spraying a huge pentagram out on the floor, surrounded by several large alchemical symbols. She then took out a large tub of table salt, and retraced her steps around the outline, coating it in a large line of white sparkly looking dust in the moonlight... This is just too perfect she thought to herself, as Marie returned with as many long twisted branches as she could carry.

"I'm not going to lie. That was fucking hard in the dark. I tripped over twice." She said angrily. "That pentagram looks mint, by the way." Quickly changing the subject. "What do the symbols mean?" She asked inquisitively.

"They are all Alchemy symbols, but not for one particular thing... Sooo basically if anyone looks them up they are all from different elements of witchcraft, but none of them connect. Some are from curses; some are from healing spells, some from love spells. It will send anyone who tries to research it a complete headache."

"Nice, I love it. What are we doing with these? She asked, dumping all the branches on the floor. They're pretty heavy." She said laughing.

"We make the pentagram the same as on the floor. We have string to tie the branches together, and then I'm going to nail it gently to the tree above her head... There is one thing we haven't discussed: who's holding her and who's killing her?"

"You do it; she's the seventh one, so I will hold her... You can slit her throat!" Marie said calmly.

Chapter 9 - Murder at midnight

The time is midnight, the moon is full and glaring, and an old oak tree stands in the light opposite the ruined statue and grave site. Rebecca's body lay slumped and asleep next to the tree, carefully and quietly the wooden pentagram was nailed above her head. Rebecca stirred a few times but didn't wake. The scene was set.

Marie gets into position to one side of Rebecca's sleeping body and holds up her head. Jet rooting through the backpack, to find a small double edged athame that glinted in the light.

"Hold her steady." Jet said with a determined look on her face. She raised the dagger high in the air to one side and with one swift swipe brought it across Rebecca's neck. A gaping hole appeared in her throat, blood oozing from the wound and gushing at one side. Rebecca awoke with a few short gargled breaths, and the words. "You bitch!" With that she was dead.

"She still had to get that last fucking word in; you should have brought some real witchcrafty stuff. It would have been more climactic than that." Marie said, riddled with sarcasm. Can I let go now?" She said with an attitude.

"Let me get rid of these ropes first then you can, for now hold her head still." Jet started untying the ropes. This task is quite hard when you're trying not to get covered with blood. "Right. Now you can let go." As Marie let go Rebecca's head slumped down forward onto her blood soaked chest.

"Don't take those gloves off until we are back at camp," Jet instructed Marie, while collecting all the tools they had used, wrapping the athame carefully in a cloth, so as to not get blood in or on her bag.

"Right... Spray can. Check. Ropes. Check. Mallet and nails. Check..."

"Tits and ass. Check." Marie said laughing, "Sorry I just had to say that. She laughs louder.

"This bits fucking serious woman! We can leave no evidence or trace that we had anything to do with this; she went for a piss didn't come back. So we go looking for her... Camera on, and we come across this scene. We then call the police. It's elaborate and you're going to have to do a lot of explaining yourself a hundred and one times, so our stories need to be straight. Got it?"

"Ooooooo." She laughs "I get it. I get it ok. Someone's cranky. She covers her mouth trying not to laugh any more, when she sees the look on Jet's face serious and stern.

"Seriously I do not want to go to prison so you had better sort your shit out woman. I know we share the same crazy ideas, and neither of us seem to get emotional about this stuff, but still this is a big one, we have to do this right. I mean can you handle it if this shit makes the news?"

"Jesus I never even thought of that! Ok I have my shit together boss, what do we need to do?"

"We need to go back to camp, have a fire, burn the rope, gloves and anything you got blood on clothes wise. I got some splatter on my shirt so that will have to go."

"I came out clean with no blood... See." She holds her gloved hands up in the air.

"Good but they still have your fingerprints on the inside of them. They have to go!"

"You have watched way too much crime stuff dude. Honestly you should have been a PI." She said laughing.

"Right on that note. Let's head back to the camp and get that fire going; we have everything packed, so we leave now. I also feel a bit hypoglycaemic so could do with some sugar after that."

"Ok let's go." Marie understood.

As Jet and Marie walked back to camp, they discussed the ins and outs of the story and how it would work, getting the story down so that they knew what the other would say. On returning they observed a small fox playing in the bushes just ahead of them.

"Awwww he's beautiful." They said in unison.

"Don't you just want to pet him or her?" Marie said in a whispered tone.

"Yeah but we have to leave him be, if he's hungry he may come to the camp. Brr it's gone cold, you get the kettle on, and I will make us a fire," Jet began making a criss cross of sticks, and chunks of wood, above a generous amount of fire lighter blocks. Sticking a few bits of paper in she then added flame... Whoosh up it went crackling and popping as the smaller sticks caught light.

"Perfect. Much warmer now." She said smiling and warming her hands, removing the gloves and watching them bubble and melt in the fire. Jet then opened the bag, wiped down the bloody athame and added the cloth to the flames, followed shortly by the rope and Marie's gloves.

"I have been dying to get them off my hands; I hate rubber gloves of any kind."

"Better than your finger prints on stuff though right?"

"Yeah that is true." She chuckled passing Jet a hot steaming cup of tea. "Can I poke the fire?"

"You can do better than that, I am still going hypo, so ta da... Marshmallows." She runs to get them from the tent.

"You beauty bless ya, I love marshmallows. Are they the big puffy ones?"

"Yep and I brought wooden forks too, just chuck them in the fire when you're done, less mess to take home and no washing up." They both laugh.

They both sat warming by the fire, tea in one hand marshmallows in the other, mesmerized by the beautiful flames within. Jet broke the silence.

"I need to go bury that spray can somewhere or maybe up in a tree hole would be better?" Jet said questionably.

"Tree would be better. Give me ten minutes and I will be back. Where's my torch gone... Found it. Right I will be back in no more than ten minutes," With those words she darted off into the direction of the toilet stick, and off into the woods.

While on that mission, Marie sat and rolled smokes, munching on all the goodies she could find in the tent box, and washing them down with a warm cup of tea, taking her trainers off and toasting her feet by the fire. This is the life she thought. I could live out here under the stars without a care in the world, it's so peaceful and calm with only the forest noises in the background. But two quiet Marie thought to herself, rooting around in the tent she found a small speaker and put on some reggae music in the background. At that point Jet came back from her trip to the woods out of breath.

"The can is gone. I put it in a hole half way up a tree and I'm pretty sure it was a squirrel home, so they may have less room now, but it's wedged in good and proper."

"Awwww did you have to destroy a squirrel's home?" Marie asked, saddened.

"I love animals dude but... Prison... Squirrels... Hmm ya know less prison option is better in my eyes. Anyway it's been about twenty minutes now, so we should go look for her, you got the camera ready?"

"Ready!" She Exclaimed. Putting her trainers back on her feet. "Camera is now... Three, two, one. On."

"Rebecca's been ages now; I'm quite worried about her." Jet said, concerned.

"You think we should go look for her?" Marie said, rehearsed.

"Yeah let's go together torches on. Use the flash on the camera too, so we have more light." The two headed off into the woods following the toilet stick until they reached the camping loo.

"Well she's not here. Where the hell could she be?" The question left open ended.

"REBECCA!" They shout in unison "REBECCA!"

"Let's go on a bit further, maybe the loo pot is full or something and she went further out?" Marie said from behind the camera.

"Rebecca! Rebecca! Can you hear us? Where are you?" Jets questions were only answered by silence. As they walked further on into the woods they reached the clearing with Rebecca's body, just as they left it half hour ago.

"Oh my god Rebecca." Jet said acting concerned. Marie squealing in the background.

"We need to call the police. Now!" Jet said, bending down to check Rebecca's pulse. "She's dead."

"Our phones are back at camp, they have no signal until we get back on the main road." Marie thinking quickly on improvisation." Jet not looking happy.

Oh my god woman you're still filming. She's dead, turn the camera off. We need to head back now and call the police."

"Ok Ok I'm turning it off now, let's go." Marie said, turning the camera off. The two headed back to camp to collect what bits they needed.

"I'm still going hypo with all this walking. I need more sugar when we get back before we walk to the main road, I also need to stick the athame back in my sheath and strap it to my ankle." Jet began to worry that her diabetes may mess up this plan, she wasn't used to having such low blood sugars all the time.

Chapter 10 - That was unexpected

Back at the campsite Marie looked smug and she knew something… "Here is a fact for you. Did you know that Diabetes kills 3.4 million people a year or so?" She said shocked.

"Yeah it's a bad illness to live with too." Jet said rustling around in the tent. "Where's all the munch gone? I can't find any sweets. Have you got the marshmallows out there?" Jets hypo taking hold and her body beginning to shake profusely.

"Sit yourself down in the tent, and I will look for you." Marie said while shuffling about. "You realise that there is none left… I ate them all."

"What the hell Marie. Why would you do that I'm a fucking diabetic." Jet now fuming at the thought of having to walk all the way back, while her whole body shook. She tries to stand feeling the effects coming on thick and fast.

"Just lay down and let go Jet, you know you want to." Marie said slyly.

"What are you on about woman? I can't get up, you're going to have to help me."

"Or NOT!" Marie said laughing "One hundred unit's right? That's what you gave Sarah, and that's what I gave you. Jabbed you right in the ass when we were out looking for Rebecca; I was really surprised how easy it was, still had the gloves on and everything. You may end on seven victims, but I am only just getting started. I don't want to stop. You are my first." Marie said, looking smug with herself.

"What the hell Marie. You're topping me off after years of friendship, and all we have been through together in life. Why? Why me?" Jet knew at this point there was no hope. The phones had no signal, there was not enough sugar in the world to take this off and she knew what was going to happen. "This is going to be brutal, I'm going to fit, then go into a coma and die. At least when I killed Sarah she was asleep, and didn't have to go through all this... This is just cruel you bitch."

"You have taught me well though my friend. The student becomes the master. All I have to do is walk back to the main road and call the police. You killed all these people, and then killed yourself out of guilt. It's poetic really." Marie's smugness now coming across like this was planned all along in her head.

"And how? ... Just... Do you think you're going to get away with all this?" Where's the planning?" Jet said, now shaking uncontrollably on the sleeping bag in the tent. "You will never get away with it like I did." Jet began to cry, something she hadn't done in years.

"The explanation written in your suicide note says otherwise." She said laughing. "I copied three of your kills together to make one. You killed all these people including Rebecca, and then hot shot yourself for a suicide with your own medication. The letter in the bottom of your bag says it all."

"Fu...ck... I...Need... Sug." Jet could not finish the sentence. She lay there knowing her future was doomed. Marie had done everything right. The shot of insulin from Sarah, but hot shooting like Matt, and the suicide note from Sue and David. It was all perfect. "All... I Can... Sa...y is... You did... Well... I... Lo...ve... You!" Jet said as her body went into convulsions and writhed around in agony. Her whole frame having a large shudder, and then she crashed."

"Coma time." Marie chuckled to herself. "I think I got time for a brew and a smoke before walking home, I must remember..." She took the video camera, and proceeded to delete all footage from the memory card.

"You did all this, you crazy cow." She said looking at Jet's comatose and now lifeless body. Marie smiled to herself knowing that in half an hour. Jet would be dead!

Finishing her smoke and brew, Marie left the campsite exactly as it stood and headed off down the lane, Taking photos of the old Manor house, and surrounding area with her phone. She wanted to hold a little souvenir to take home. Thinking of how she had suggested every killing. Jet was never in control, she thought to herself, as she mumbled her explanations aloud.

"Sarah was a leech on society, Sue and David were selfish assholes, Shell should have never put the dog to sleep, Matt was a narcissistic drug addict, Mum was just a complete bitch, and Rebecca took away my oldest friend. I'm glad you killed them all. I love you too Jet and I am going to miss you the most."

Marie had thought of everything, and was wildly thinking of all the other people that had wronged her in life. "They all need to die." She said to herself quietly. Jet would be dead by the time anyone reached her, and all she had to do was cry and wail emotionally at the police, and this would all be over. Surely no one was going to question it, once Marie had spilled the beans about all seven murders; no one would question the suicide at the end. Her mind wandered on to new victims and new ways to commit the murders, she wondered if Jets Mum would let her have all the books she owned, as there was enough herbalism and witchcraft stuff in there to kill a small tribe.

"Jet's Mum." Suddenly the realisation kicked in of how devastated she would be about her daughter's death. Although knowing the woman well, she would probably take her under her wing as her own... Hmm, a new Mum. A kind Mum.

Marie thought to herself. It was a very appealing thought.

Reaching the top of the lane near the main road, her phone signal sprung to life. She dialled 999.

Chapter 11 - All is well?

Three months later.

Barbara Green was a wonderful woman; she truly has a heart of gold and would help anyone in need. She had taken the death of her daughter hard, and as Marie first thought she had gravitated towards her. After Marie lost her mum Barbara rallied round for donations, food packages, and lifts whenever they were needed. Not forgetting the huge packets of treats for Bruno, that came on a monthly basis. Barbara at age seventy was a spritely working machine, refusing to slow down and age gracefully. She was the complete opposite of Marie. Teetotal, non smoker who doesn't swear or curse, in comparison to a gin swigging, chain smoking woman that swears like a trooper. Yet somehow the friendship flourished between them. Some would say better than with their own family. Jet and Barbara's relationship had always been rocky due to mental health issues, and a large age gap between the two. Whereas Marie fitted in perfectly. Young, vibrant and hard working Barbara saw the missing link, the daughter that had been taken away from her, although she longed for Jet to not have committed those crimes, she still missed her greatly and a great saddening void filled her heart.

News and media had all about died down now and moved on to the next scandalous thing to do with Covid variations. The stories surrounding Jet were short lived, although Marie made a pretty penny selling her story to several magazines and newspapers, and had even been approached about a book deal for the future. The funeral was strange though a large turnout of fans from the club, people that had followed her DJ career, several new nutters and serial killer enthusiasts, were among the crowd. Even though Jet had committed the crimes, people still seemed to love her, and didn't want to believe it happened. They showed up in tribute colours and shades of green all throughout the room. Barbara had been overwhelmed by kindness, and the show of love that people had for Jet. Marie held a wake at Jets club, Sevens had never felt so gloomy, until she reminded everyone that Jet brought back the club so people could party in the first place, and therefore that's what they must do. The people obliged and Jet's friends danced and sang the night away, to a multitude of her favourite songs. Who knows what will become of Sevens now?

Barbara pulls up in the car outside Marie's house, loaded to the rafters like a huge jumble sale, with boxes of books, guitars, lamps and ornaments. One box was labelled food stuff, and piled high with tins and jars. As usual trying to do it all herself Barbara begins to unload the car.

"Let me do that." Marie piped up. "Give it here. That's too heavy for you. Let me get Matto to come and help." Matto was

Marie's fiancé, and on being shouted away from his game of football in the main room, he begrudgingly came to help.

"What needs to go where?" He asked.

"Well there are two guitars and an amp for you there, so wherever you want to home them." Barbara said, unloading a great box of books out the back. "These are for you Marie. You may need one of the bookshelves to go with them though. If you want me to bring you them? let me know."

"Awwww bless ya Barbara thank you. That's so kind of you." Marie said with a large smile.

"I would rather it all goes to a good home and her friends rather than the tip, everything else that people don't want I am going to divide and give to charity." Tears are now rolling down her face.

"Awwww Barbara come inside, and I will make you a brew. Matto can finish doing the car."

"Thank you Marie, I would like that. Do I finally get to meet Bruno, and give him some treats?"

"You can give him all the treats, loves and fusses that you like darling. He will love you for it, just watch he doesn't get too excited and hurt himself. He's a dopey bugger."

After a few hours of stories and general chit chat Barbara says she had better be getting back, and the group part for the evening. Marie sat contemplating, looking through some of the herbal books that had been left to her. Remembering that Jet had told her about the common foxglove and all the weird and wonderful things it could do. I wonder if I could make LSD? She thought to herself. Or poison? The thoughts then leading to who she would kill next and why? Did she need a reason anymore? All she knew is that life was dull and mundane; she needed that excitement in her life, but that there was also so much more she had to learn.

Two Years Later.

Marie had not put aside her thoughts; rather she had channelled and focused them onto the next level of excitement. Within the two years Marie and Matto had gotten married, paid off most of their mortgage, and settled down in bliss. The house and garden flourished, with fresh herbs, vegetables and flowers of all kinds. Marie had become quite green fingered since inheriting Jets book collection. Although a darker side had appeared in their marriage. Matto was struggling with addiction, and by that I don't mean drugs or alcohol. His addiction was football; you name it the man was football mad. If he wasn't playing it, he was watching it, if not watching it then talking about it. It was beginning to grind Marie's gears after so many years; she could hear the noise from the living room.

"YEEEES! GET IN! ONE NIL." Matto shouted. A large sigh coming from Marie. "One nil, one nil, one niiiiiiiiil." He sang. Football was the true love of Matto's life, and Marie was feeling it big time.

Marie opened the patio doors, and went into the garden with Bruno, Picking several flowers and herbs she filled her little bowl, with tomatoes and mint leaves she was so proud of growing.

"Do you want a brew before tea?" She shouted from the garden, Matto had the football on so loud he was oblivious to the question. Marie returned to the house shouting. "Oi. I said do you want a brew before tea?" She repeated loudly from the door of the main room.

"One nil. One nil, one nil." Matto sang in her face. "We are winning and there's only twenty minutes left to go till full time,

Whoooo." The question still unanswered, as he turned back to the TV and re submerged himself in the action.

"You know what? You're a dickhead." Marie said laughing and walking back to the kitchen, she grabbed a handful of herbs from the side, and proceeded to grind them in the pestle and mortar. "I will show you. I am not being second best to anything." She said under her breath, as the contents were making a thick paste. She then added a few drops of boiling water from the kettle, and began to stir; a strange green liquid began to emerge. Marie then took a teaspoon and added two to the cup. Adding the tea bag and two spoons of sugar. Wait let's make it three she thought, he has a sweet tooth. The boiling water then poured into the mix, making sure she squished the bag real hard, to make the tea as strong as possible. Last but not least the milk went in.

"Looks normal… Smells normal." She said to herself, walking through to the other room.

"Here your highness, brew is made." She said sarcastically walking off back into the kitchen. Matto was still engrossed in the last ten minutes of the game. Taking a huge gulp of tea he shouts.

"Ouch Jesus that's hot." Like it hadn't just come out of a boiling kettle. He blows on the surface and try's again, slurping the contents slower this time as to not burn his mouth. Placing the cup down on the table he outbursts again. "Oh My God! Two nil now, whooooo yeah. We have won this. Get in!" He walks into the kitchen brew in hand. Smiling from ear to ear.

"How's your tea?" Marie said, smiling to herself.

"Perfection. Thank you my dear." He said while dialling a friend to talk about the game. Give it ten minutes, she thought. You will be shitting like a trooper. She giggled to herself.

Matto could be heard pacing throughout the house, calling different people but having the same conversation every time. Red cards this, and referees that. Marie's blood began to boil, but on the third rendition of the same story she heard it.

"Aw man I have to go; I seriously need to take a dump. I will call you back." Marie now giggling profusely as Matto ran upstairs to the bathroom. She could hear him moaning and groaning from downstairs, as she popped on some background tunes to drown out the noise.

About twenty minutes had gone by, and the lasagne in the oven was nearly done. Marie turned down the tunes and shouted upstairs. "I am dishing up babe." There was no reply. Marie turned off the oven and removed the large tray. "Babe can you hear me? Food is ready!" There was still no response. Marie, now worried, headed upstairs to see what was wrong. It would appear that after his ordeal with the toilet bowl, he had gone to lie down and had fallen asleep. "Bloody typical." Marie said as Bruno jumped on the bed beside him. "Babe wake up. Food's ready." She said, shaking him gently. His body flopped over, now more on his back, legs still sideways on. "You sleep like the dead. WAKE UP!" She shouted. Bruno begins to cry and whinge, pouring at Matto's legs and the covers. It was then she realised he wasn't breathing. "Oh shit! Babe! She shook him aggressively. Still no response. She quickly dials 999.

"Emergency services, how may I help you? What assistance do you require?" The woman on the other end said calmly.

"Oh my god erm, a practical joke has gone wrong I think my husband might be dead." She said in floods of tears. After giving her address and details, an ambulance and police were dispatched. Matto had suffered a massive cardiac arrest, and was pronounced dead. Marie took one look at the officer, and broke down in floods of tears. "It was only a joke. It was only meant to give him diarrhoea, she sobbed. Sitting and explaining the situation, the police officer took all of the statement, and told her to sit tight. She didn't think that any further action would be taken, as it was clearly an accident, but that she would have to come down to the station to clarify everything.

Three weeks later

Marie was back home with no charges held against her, although Matto's parents had chosen to cut her out of the funeral process, due to the circumstances. As she sat in the living room sorting boxes of his belongings, she came across his favourite football shirt. That's one for the bonfire she thought, not being able to bear the thought of it being around, or someone else wearing it.

Later that night she took anything that wasn't going to charity or his friends, down to the bottom of the garden. The fire pit was stocked and ready to go, she lit the firelighter. Whoosh it started fierce. As she placed the shirt on top of the raging fire she became transfixed in the sight of the beautiful colour flames that the burning fabric gave off. Deep in thought it was then she laughed and said.

"Sod the Seven rule Jet! I'm on nine and counting."

Printed in Great Britain
by Amazon